The GREATEST in the World!

BEN CLANTON

SIMON & SCHUSTER BOOKS FOR YOUNG READERS
NEW YORK   LONDON   TORONTO   SYDNEY   NEW DELHI

# FOR THE GREATEST TRIO IN MY WORLD, THEO, GWEN, AND OLIVER!

SIMON & SCHUSTER BOOKS FOR YOUNG READERS
An imprint of Simon & Schuster Children's Publishing Division
1230 Avenue of the Americas, New York, New York 10020
© 2022 by Ben Clanton
Book design by Lucy Ruth Cummins © 2022 by Simon & Schuster, Inc.
SIMON & SCHUSTER BOOKS FOR YOUNG READERS
and related marks are trademarks of Simon & Schuster, Inc.
For information about special discounts for bulk purchases, please contact Simon
& Schuster Special Sales at 1-866-506-1949 or business@simonandschuster.com.
The Simon & Schuster Speakers Bureau can bring authors to your live event. For
more information or to book an event, contact the Simon & Schuster Speakers
Bureau at 1-866-248-3049 or visit our website at www.simonspeakers.com.
The text for this book was set in Typewrither.
The illustrations for this book were rendered in Procreate,
watercolors, potato stamps, photographs, and Photoshop.
Manufactured in China
0722 SCP
First Edition
2   4   6   8   10   9   7   5   3   1
Library of Congress Cataloging-in-Publication Data
Names: Clanton, Ben, 1988- author.
Title: The greatest in the world / Ben Clanton.
Description: First edition. | New York : Simon & Schuster Books for Young
Readers, [2022] | Series: Tater tales ; vol. 1 | Audience: Ages 6-9. | Audience:
Grades 2-3. | Summary: "Two spud siblings face off in a series of epic
challenges to prove who's "the greatest in the world"-Provided by publisher.
Identifiers: LCCN 2022003520 (print) | LCCN 2022003521 (ebook) |
ISBN 9781534493186 (hardcover) | ISBN 9781534493193 (paperback) |
ISBN 9781534493209 (ebook)
Subjects: CYAC: Graphic novels. | Contests-Fiction. | Brothers and sisters-
Fiction. | Potatoes-Fiction. | Humorous stories. | LCGFT: Graphic novels.
Classification: LCC PZ7.7.C556 Gr 2022 (print) | LCC PZ7.7.C556 (ebook) |
DDC 741.5/973-dc23/eng/20220222
LC record available at https://lccn.loc.gov/2022003520
LC ebook record available at https://lccn.loc.gov/2022003521

# CONTENTS

# CHAPTER 1
# A GREAT START

This is Rot Poe Tater. He's a mutant potato.

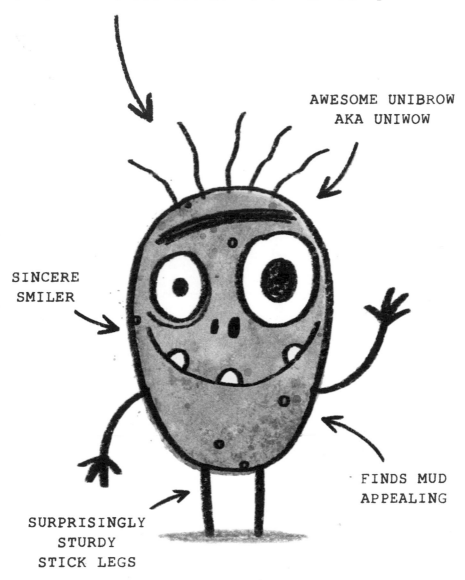

AWESOME UNIBROW
AKA UNIWOW

SINCERE
SMILER

FINDS MUD
APPEALING

SURPRISINGLY
STURDY
STICK LEGS

Early this morning Rot woke up on the right side of the garden bed. He felt good. No, more than good. Rot felt **GREAT!** Rot felt like . . .

# the GREATEST
## in the World!

And Rot felt like
singing about it . . .

## LOUDLY!

I'm the GR
in the Wo
GREATEST in
the greatest
GREATE
WO

Rot's big brother, Snot, did not feel great.
Snot felt sleepy. Sleepy and upset.

BED HEAD
HAIRDO

SNOT'S
FAVORITE
SPOT
AKA
DOTTY

TRIES TO APPEAR
THICK-SKINNED

PROUD
COUCH
POTATO

Snot felt like SHOUTING!

It's 5 A.M. !!! WHY are you making that RIDICULOUS RACKET?!

BECAUSE I FEEL **GREAT**!

GRRR-RUMP.

Like the **GREATEST** in the WORLD!

**YOU**?! The **GREATEST**?! I think NOT, ROT!

Who does Snot think is the greatest?

Himself, of course.

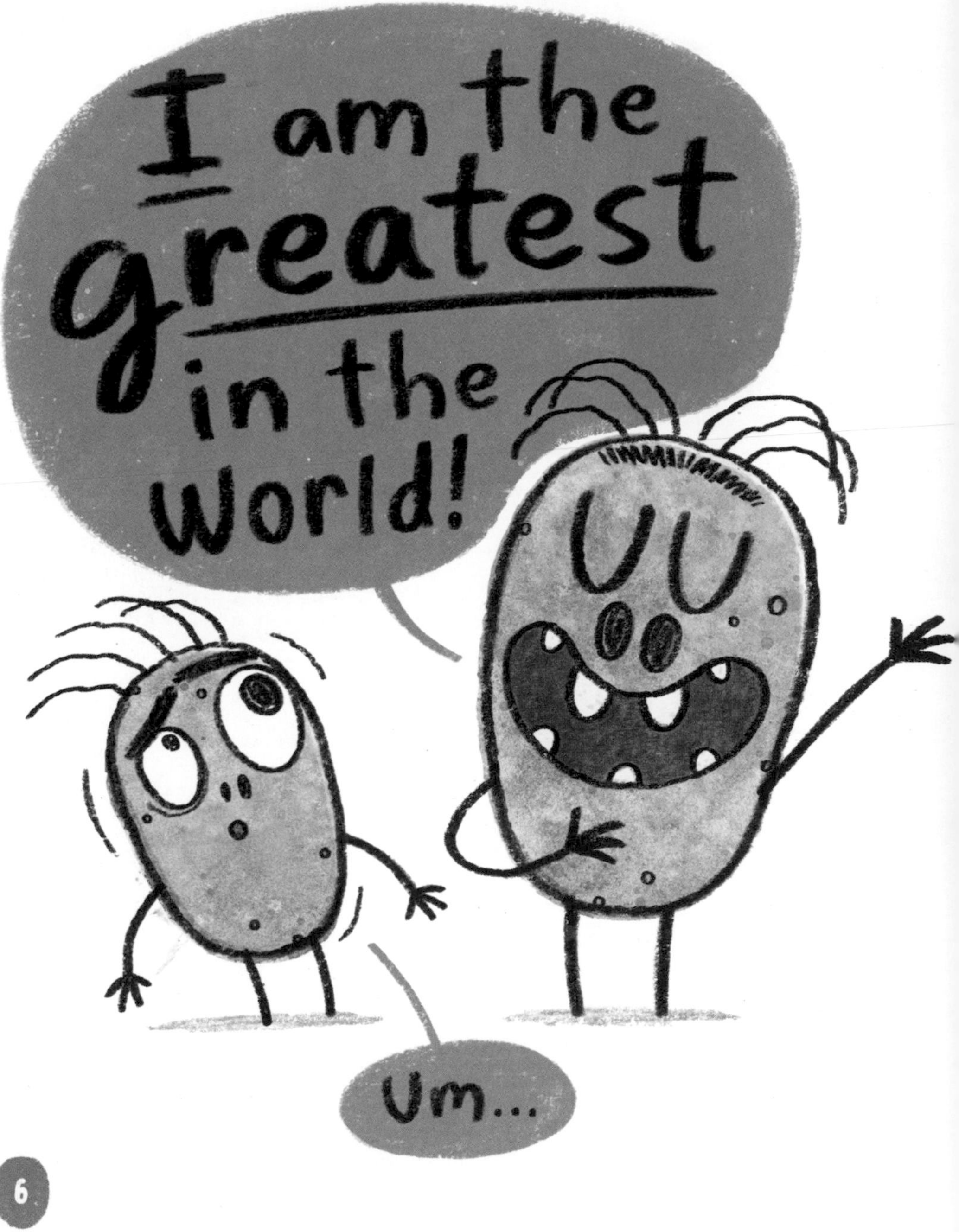
I am the greatest in the World!
Um...

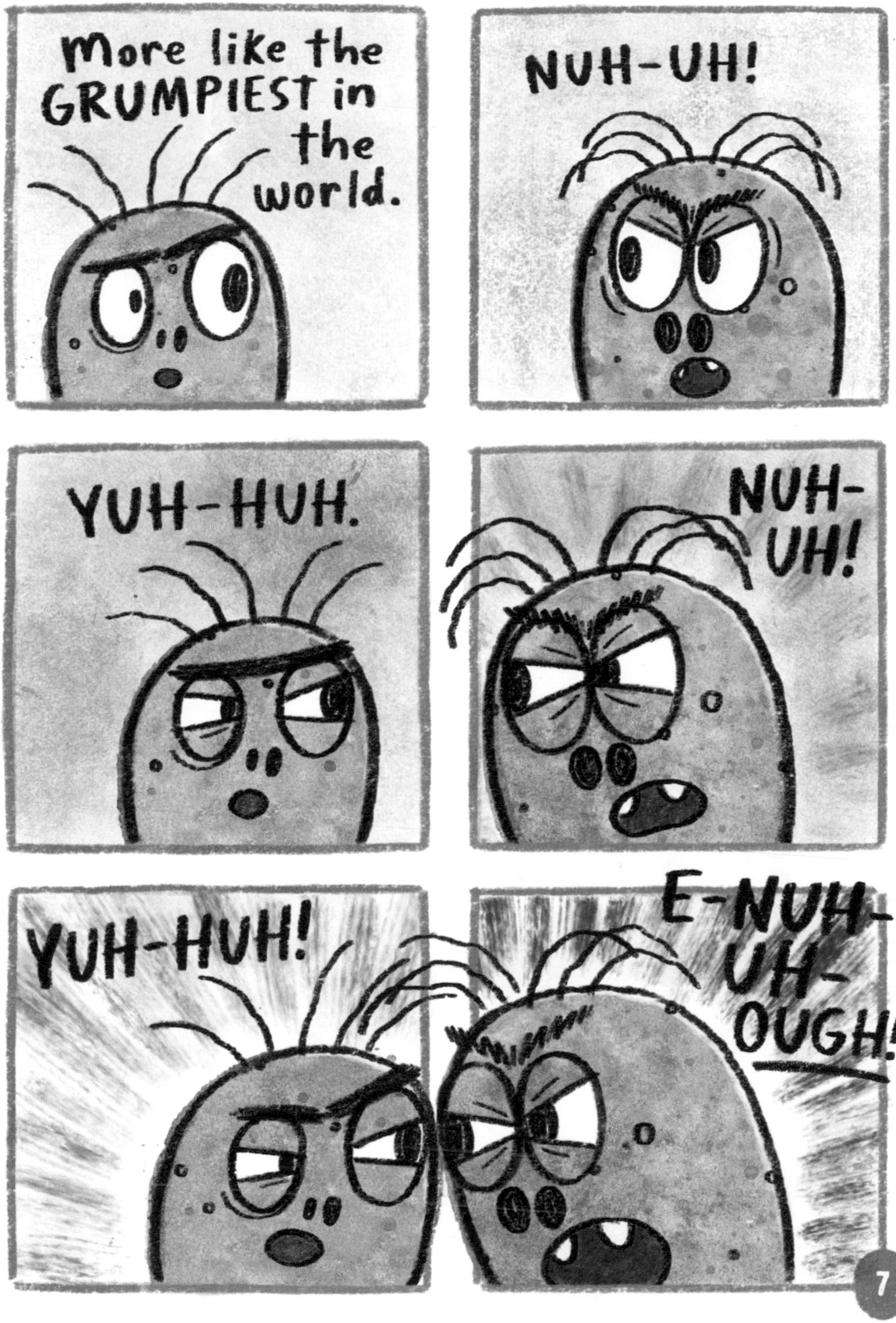
More like the GRUMPIEST in the world.
NUH-UH!
YUH-HUH.
NUH-UH!
YUH-HUH!
E-NUH-UH-OUGH!

Mutant potatoes love contests. But what kind of contest is a **GREATEST** IN THE WORLD contest?

tic-tac-

NO!

Hopscotch?

REALLY?! I had hopped you could do better than that.

I know!

Oh?

The potato sack race is considered by mutant potatoes to be one of the **GREATEST** contests. There was no way Snot could refuse.

Besides, why would he? He's never lost a potato sack race.

But who will be the judge?

Rot does not think a lot of that idea.
They need a judge who is fair and honest.
Someone like . . .

their little sister, **Tot!**

And so it is decided: a potato sack race through Barrel Bottom Bog to the top of High Hill will decide who is the **GREATEST**, once and for all.

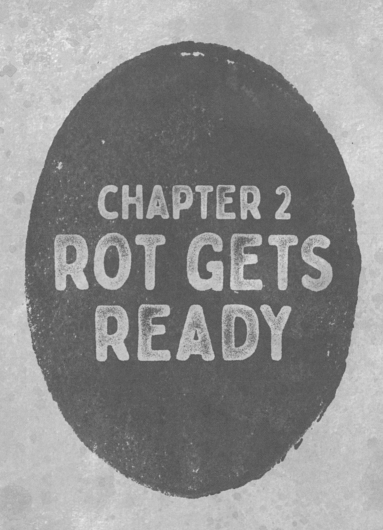

# CHAPTER 2
# ROT GETS READY

**WARNING!** You might want to plug your nose before beginning this chapter.

Rot gathers his gear for the
GREAT POTATO SACK RACE.

LUCKY SWEATBAND!
It has never
been washed.

LUCKY SOCKS!
They've never
been washed
either.

Nor has
this LUCKY
SHIRT!

Or this sort
of smelly SACK!

23

WATER BOTTLE
That is clean!

MR. FRY'S
CHAMPION
POTATOES

And a winning attitude!

Rot is ready.

Well, almost ready . . . First some stretches.

FIG. 1 THE TOES POSE-TATO

FIG. 2 THE SPLITS STANCE

FIG. 3 THE POTATO PIROUETTE-ISH POSE?

FIG. 4 THE TATER TUMBLE

Oh, also, a pep talk from Rot's best spuddy, Worm.

All your life has led to **THIS** moment! your golden opportunity to show what sort of spud you are!

Are you a half-baked potato?

NO!

A small potato?

NO!

A COUCH potato?

NO!

19

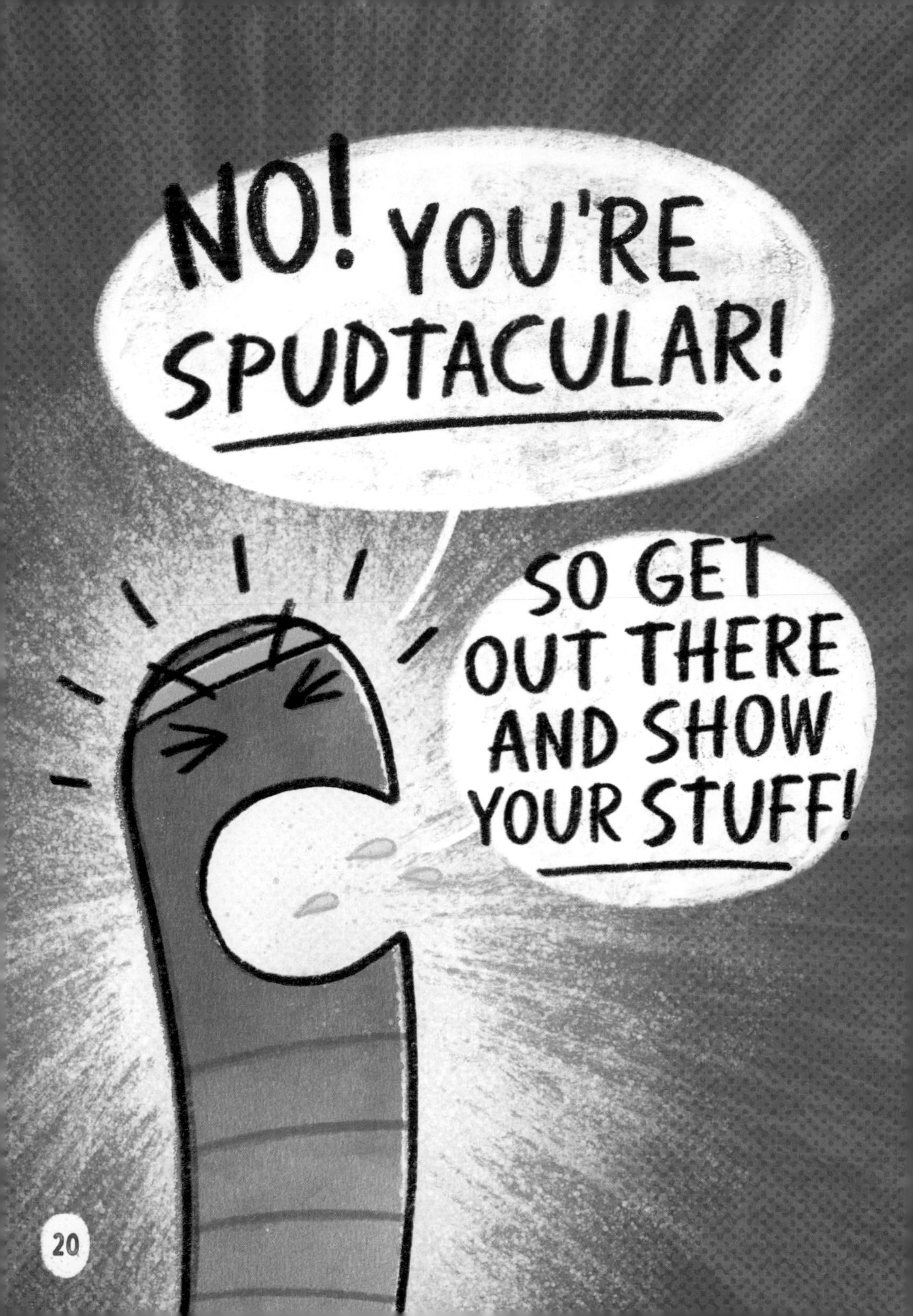
NO! YOU'RE SPUDTACULAR!
SO GET OUT THERE AND SHOW YOUR STUFF!

There! Now **ROT IS READY!**

READY TO RUMBLE!

But, wait, what about Snot?
What has Snot been doing to get ready?

Not much.

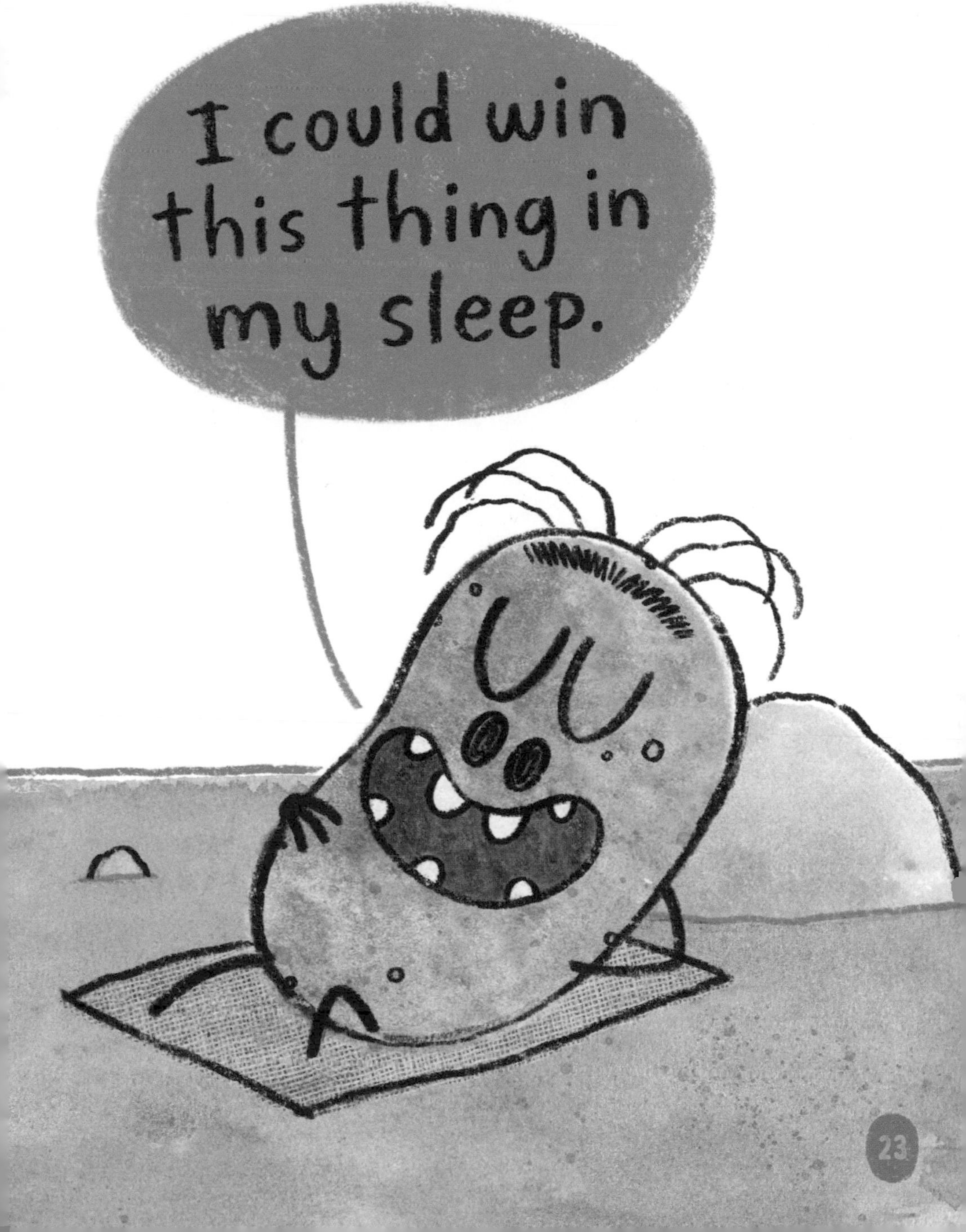
I could win this thing in my sleep.

CHAPTER 3
THE
GREAT
RACE

At last, the time for the

# Great Potato Sack Race

has come. An epic showdown between two
brothers! Who will win? Rot or Snot?

Rot puts his game face on.

So does Snot.

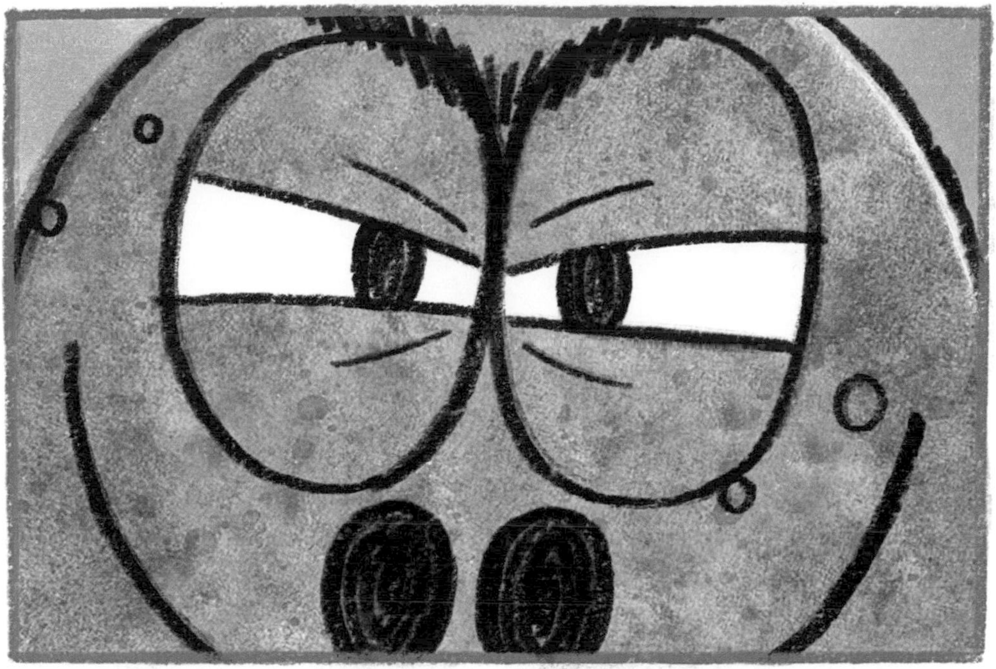

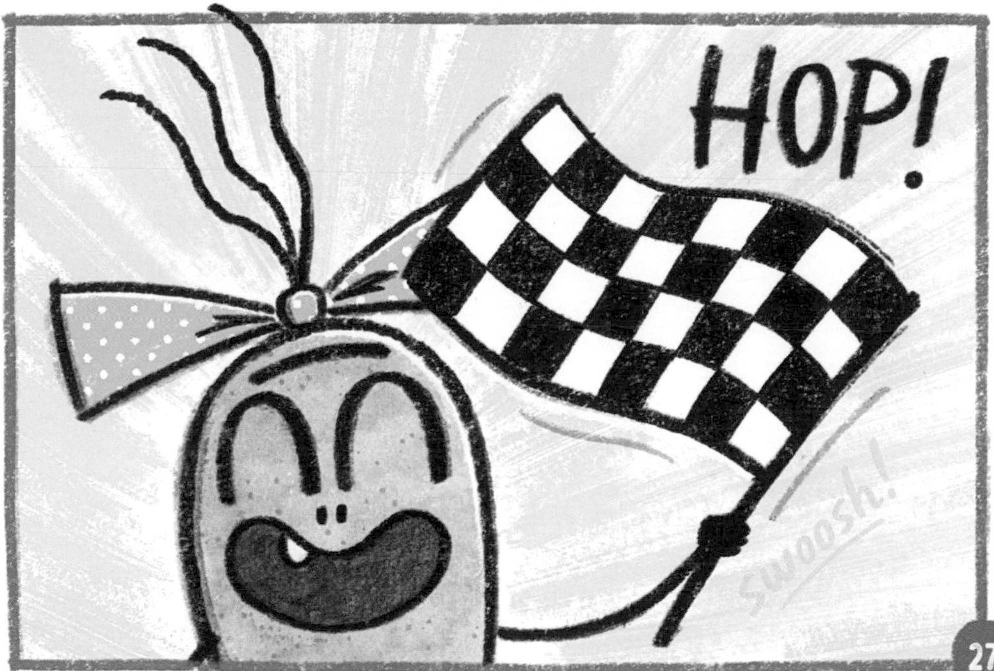
HOP!
swoosh!

Rot and Snot hop to it! So does Tot!
She hurriedly hops ahead to see who will
finish first.

Worm is already there, cheering Rot on.

But no matter how loud Worm cheers or how hard Rot tries, Snot is still bigger than his brother. Soon Snot's huge hops have him far ahead of Rot.

Snot is so far ahead that when he sees a sweet slimy spot in Barrel Bottom Bog, he decides to hop in.

Mutant potatoes love mud. They play in it, they eat it, and . . . they even sleep in it.

Snot sleeps so soundly that he doesn't hear
Rot catch up.

But WAIT! Why is Rot stopping by Snot? Will he
be a good sport and wake up his big brother?

Not so much.

Rot hops back to it! He knows he shouldn't have painted a mud mustache on Snot, but he just couldn't resist!

Now he's focused and . . .

it looks like Rot will win!

Until something disturbs Snot's slumber.

That **terribly tickly** mud mustache.

Rot is happily hopping up High Hill when it hoppins, er, happens.

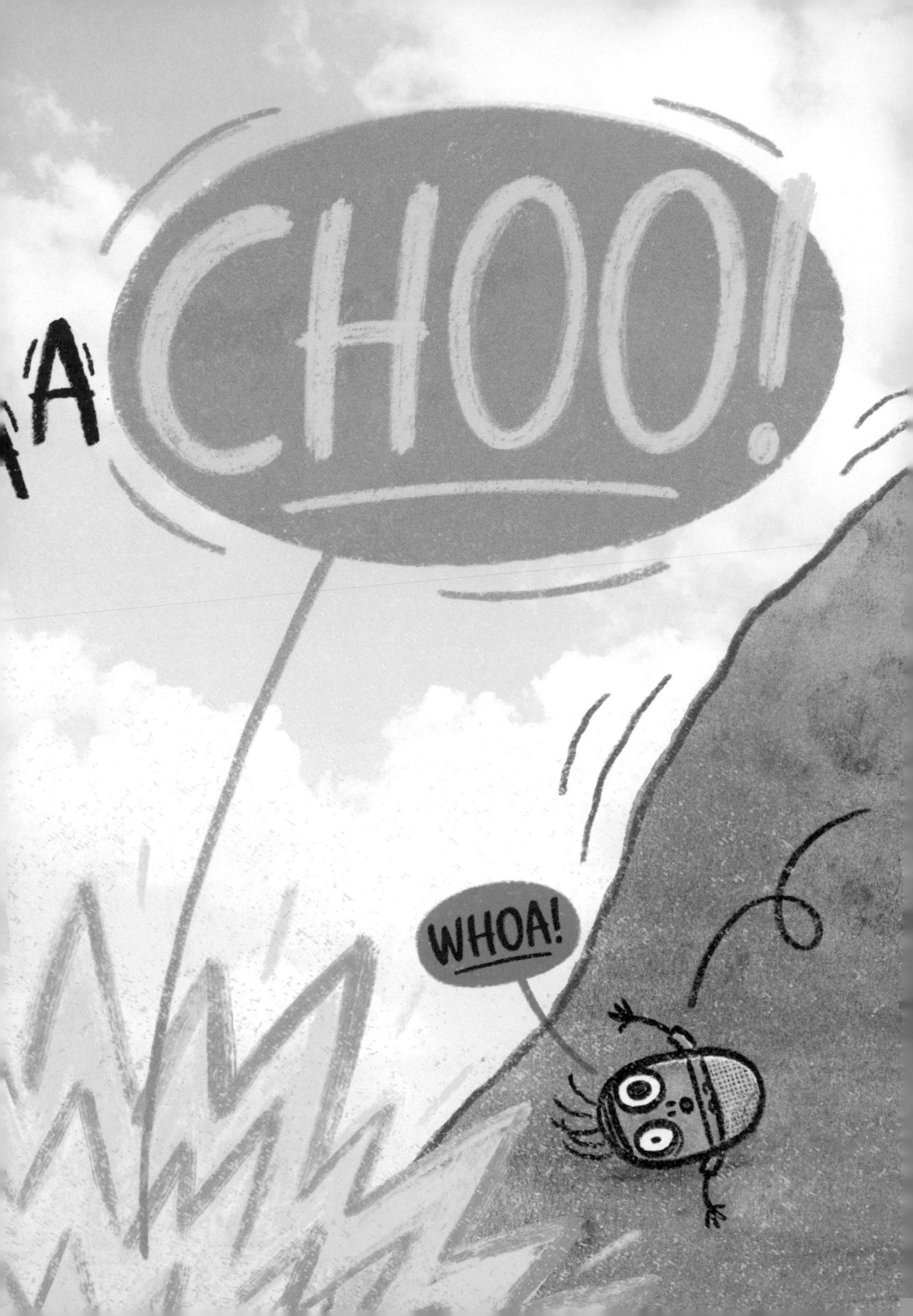
A
CHOO!
WHOA!

The **GREATEST,**
**LOUDEST** sneeze in the world!
So loud that it blows that mud mustache
right off Snot's snooty lip and shakes
the whole of High Hill . . .
causing Rot to take a tumble. . . .

And Snot to make a comeback!

A now wide-awake Snot is storming up
the steep hillside. Rot bounces back up,
but Snot is gaining ground.

Now they're neck and neck!

SNOT PULLS AHEAD! He raises his arms,
certain of his success. Rot digs deep
for his greatness and makes a determined
lunge for the finish line.

And the winner is . . . OH MY! It's a . . .

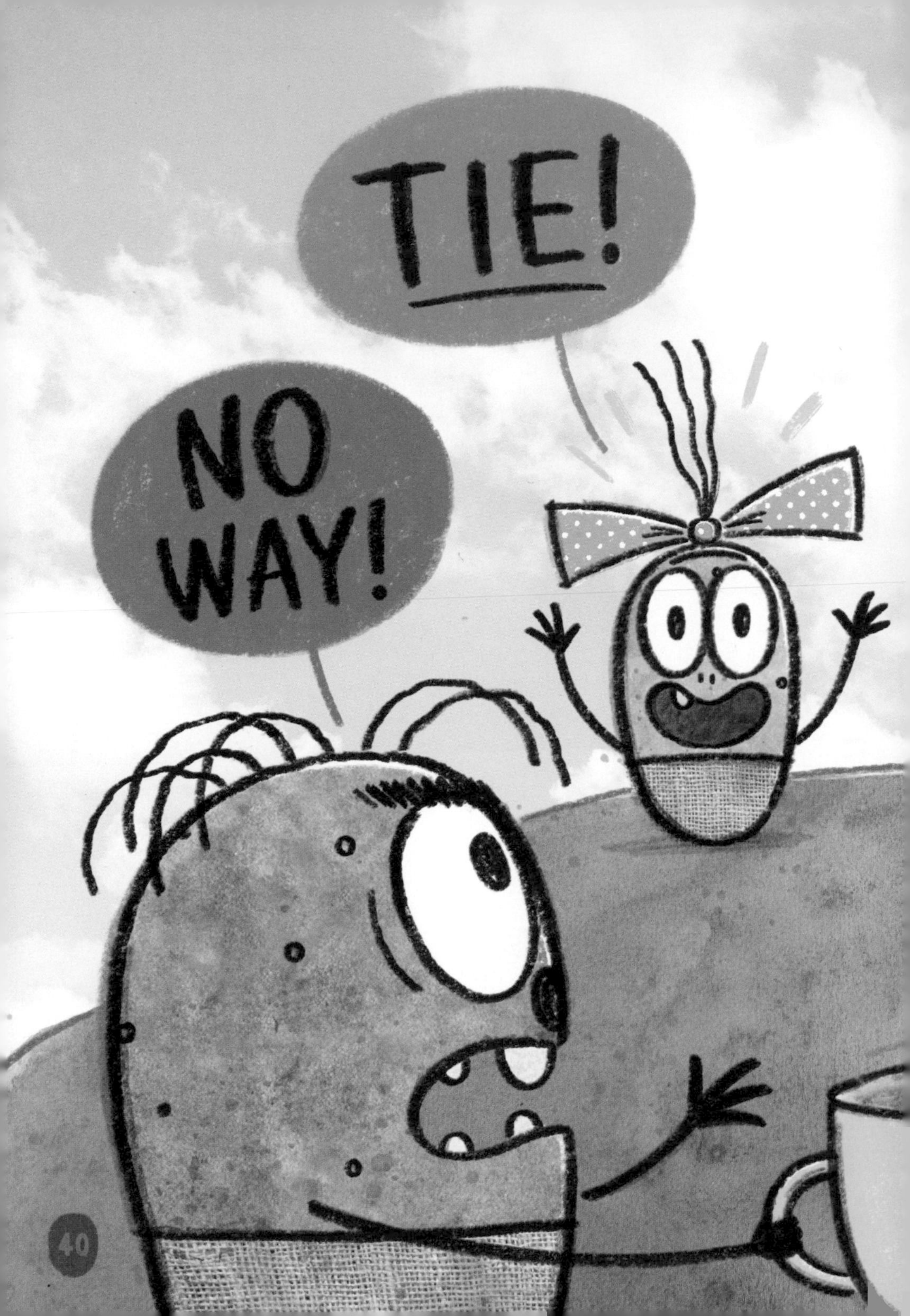
TIE!
NO WAY!

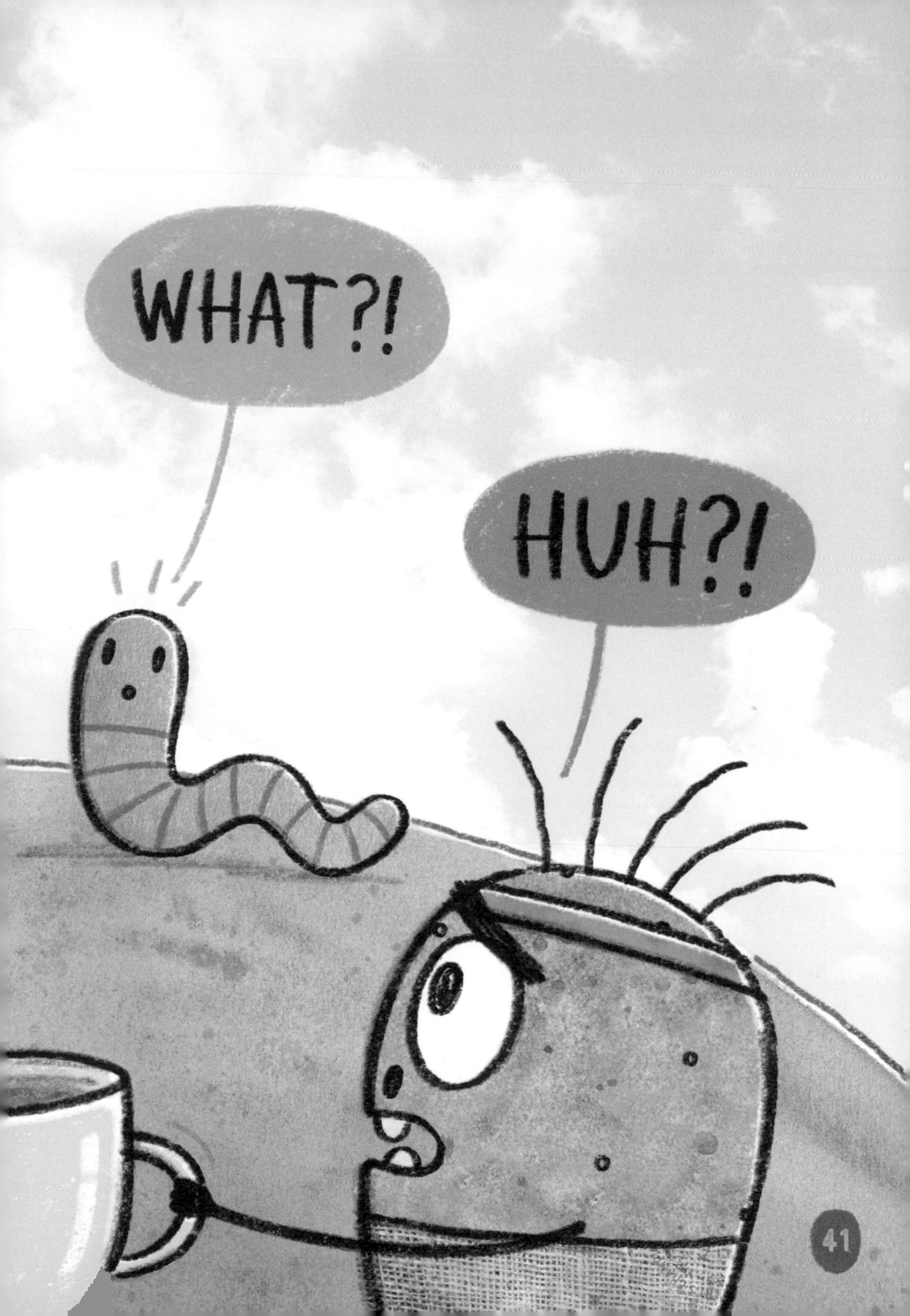
WHAT?!
HUH?!

# CHAPTER 4
# HOT POTATO HILL

Snot is stunned. Snot is upset. Snot insists that he be declared the victor.

But Tot is the judge. And she will not be moved.

She decides that there will be a second contest to determine the **GREATEST** in the World!

This time picking the contest is no contest. The top of High Hill is the perfect place for a legendary competition beloved by mutant potatoes all over. A challenge steeped in tradition, rich with history.

HOT POTATO HILL!

Rumor has it that the game originates long ago, when a mutant potato named Hashley Brown stood too closely to a campfire one night on top of High Hill. . . .

Hashley tried putting out the fire by rolling. Soon she was tumbling down High Hill with all her spuddies running after, trying to help.

It is said that by the bottom of the hill, Hashley Brown was laughing loudly.

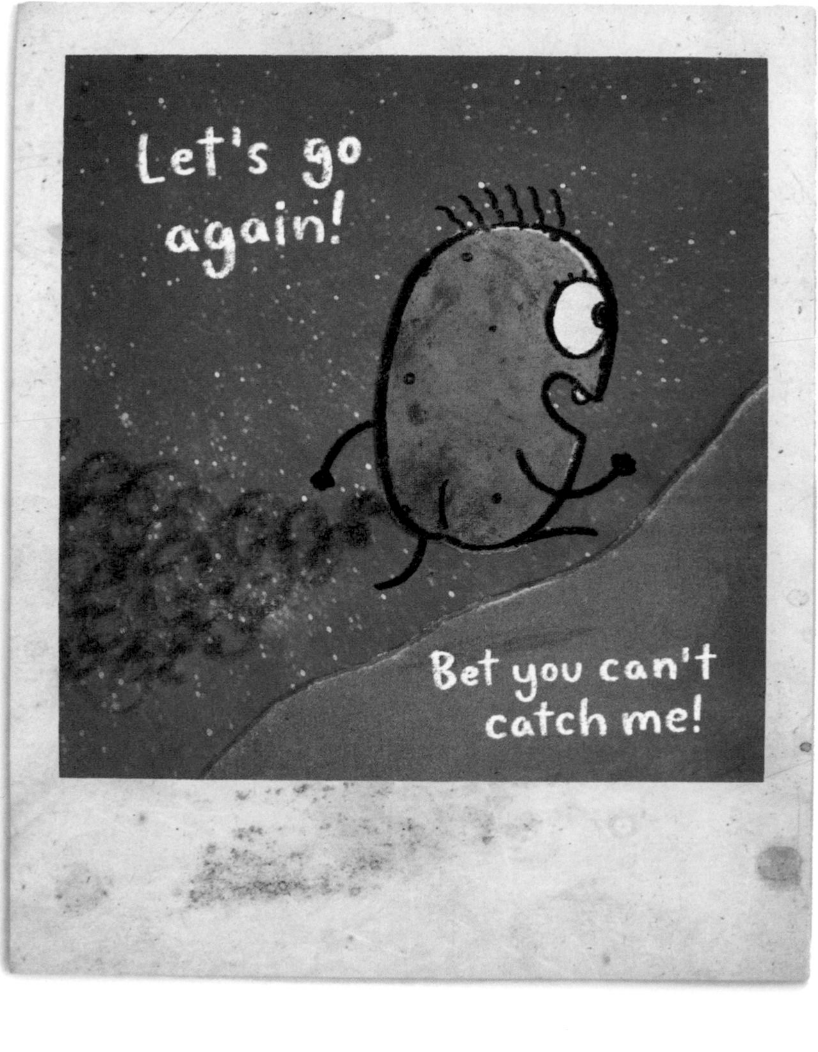
Let's go again!
Bet you can't catch me!

So began the **GREATEST** of games.

And this is how you play it:

# HOT POTATO HILL INSTRUCTIONS

1. Find the BEST, **BIGGEST** hill possible. Go to the top of it.

2. Pick someone to be the HOT POTATO.

3. Everyone chases the HOT POTATO down the hill by rolling after them.

4. The HOT POTATO gets a four-second head start. Those chasing the HOT POTATO must shout out "one potato, two potato, three potato, FOUR!" before starting to roll.

5. You win by catching the HOT POTATO.

Tot starts rolling down the hill.

Then Snot starts swirly-whirly-twirling after,
and Rot rumble-tumble-rolls not far behind.

Rot and Snot rapidly roll after their little sister, Tot. But Tot is not easily caught. She twists and turns like a top! She never comes to a stop!

Rot reaches for her, but Tot slides to the side. Snot lurches at Tot, but she leap-rolls away.

The entire time Tot sings . . .

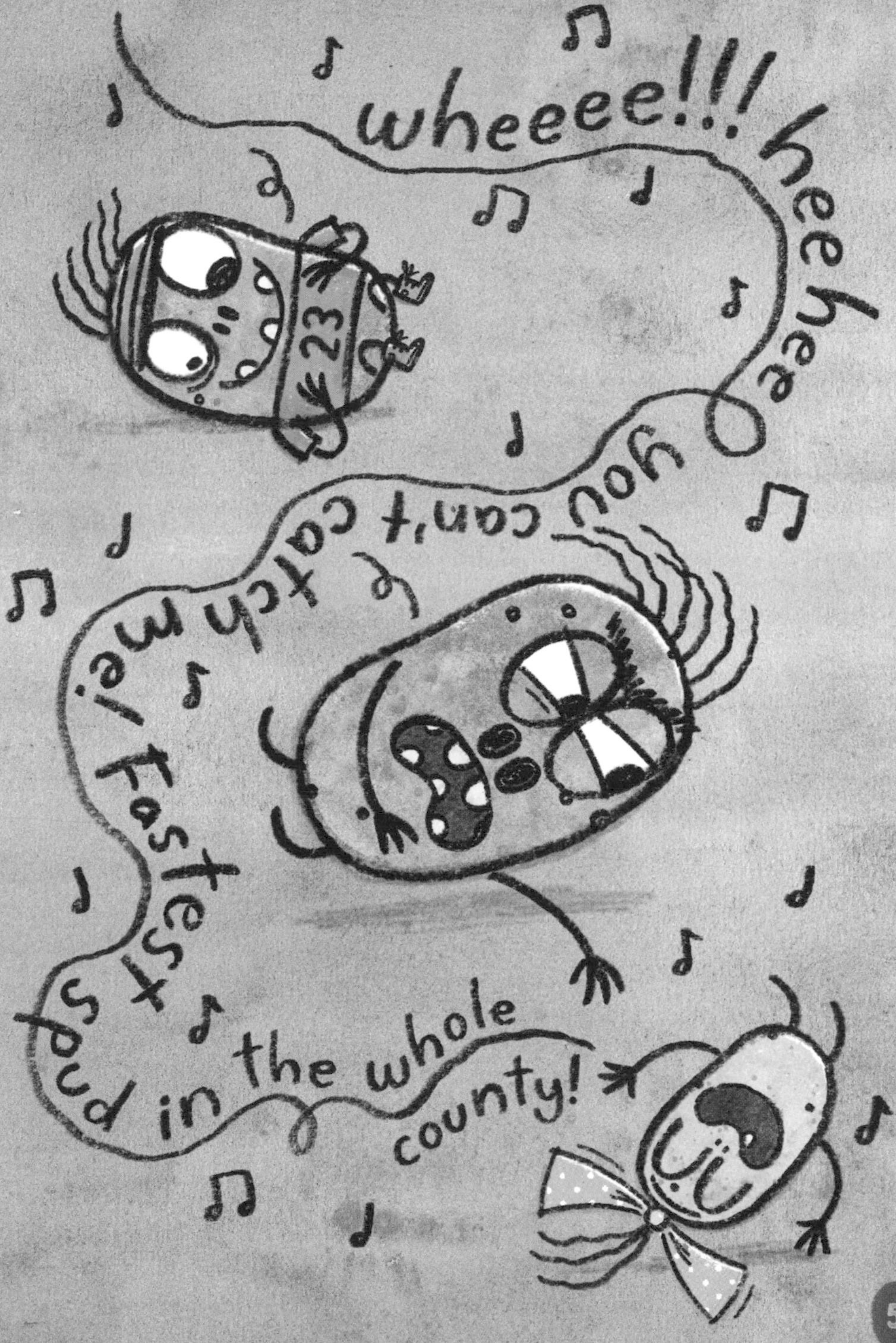

wheeee!!! heehee
you can't catch me! Fastest spud in the whole county!

And sure enough, Tot rolls
all the way to the bottom of
High Hill without being caught.

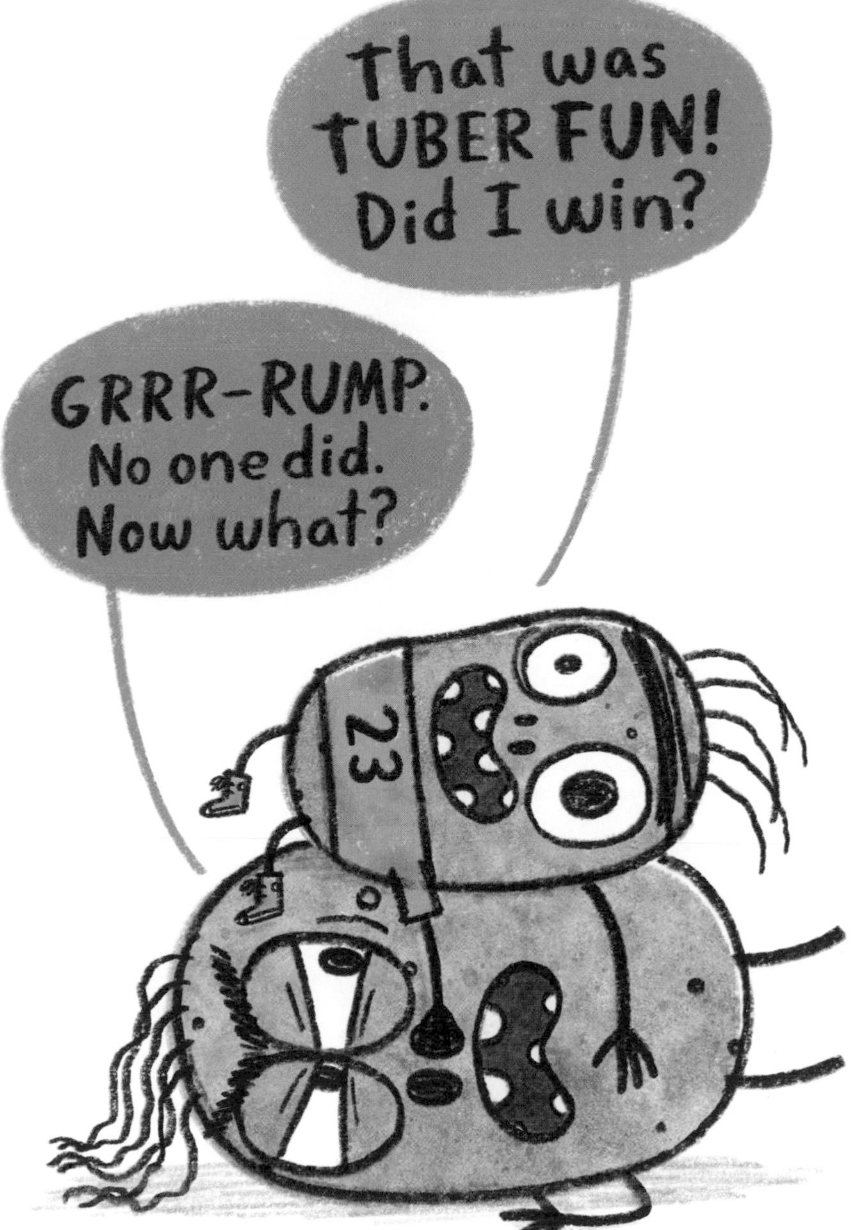
That was TUBER FUN! Did I win?
GRRR-RUMP. No one did. Now what?
23

# CHAPTER 5
# THE LAST LAUGH

Since neither Snot nor Rot won, it is decided that there needs to be a third and final competition. Something to determine who is the greatest, once and for all! But what should it be?

hee! hee!

hee!

Tot is still laughing after her triumph, and spuddenly, Rot has an idea.

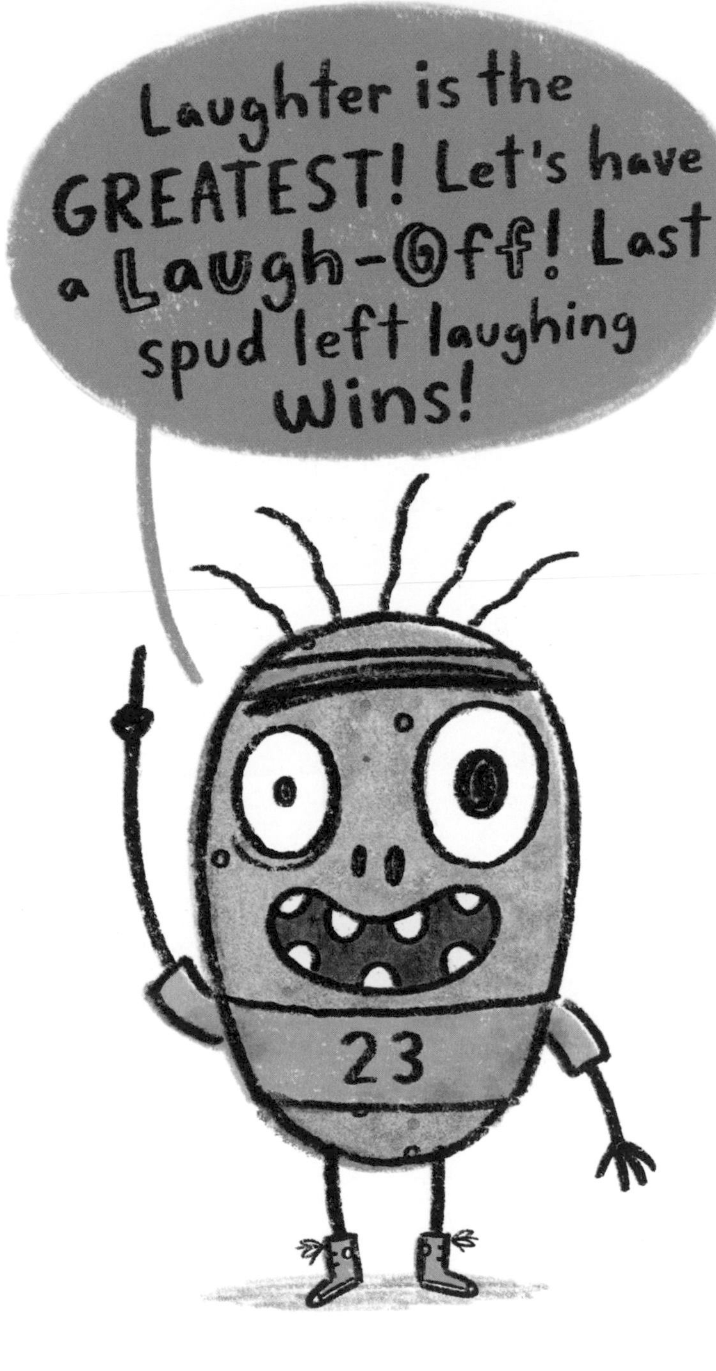
Laughter is the GREATEST! Let's have a Laugh-Off! Last spud left laughing wins!
23

Tot likes this idea a lot! As for Snot . . .

Snot starts out strong with a **GREAT** guffaw!

Rot responds with a gurgling giggle.

Snot comes back with a classic: the *EVIL* laugh.

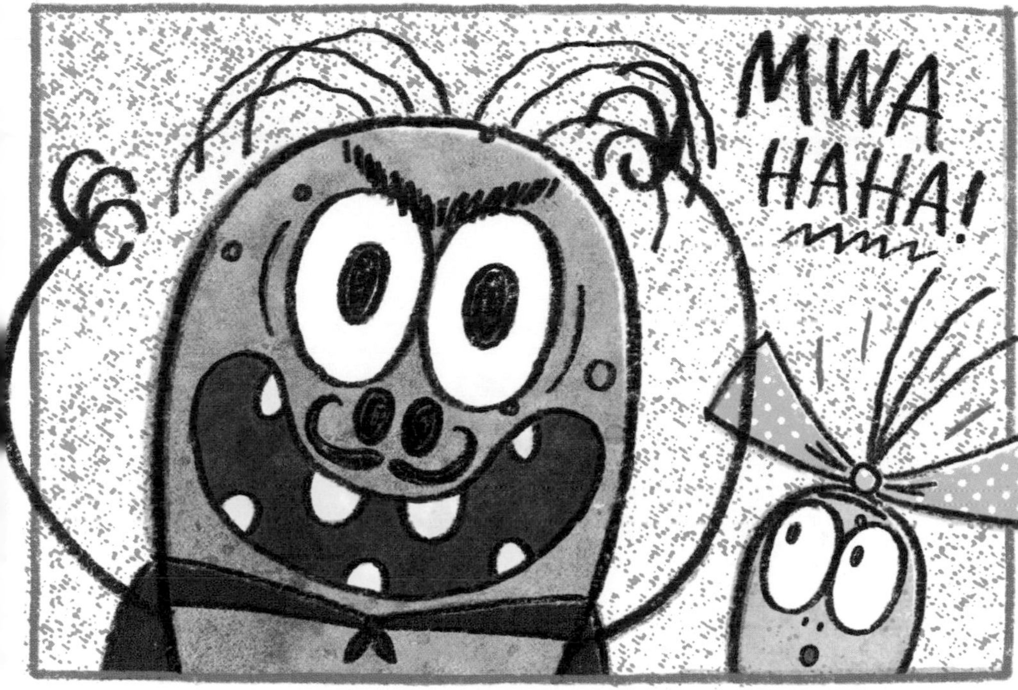
MWA HAHA!

Not to be outdone, Rot shakes out a superb Santa laugh (aka the belly-jelly laugh).

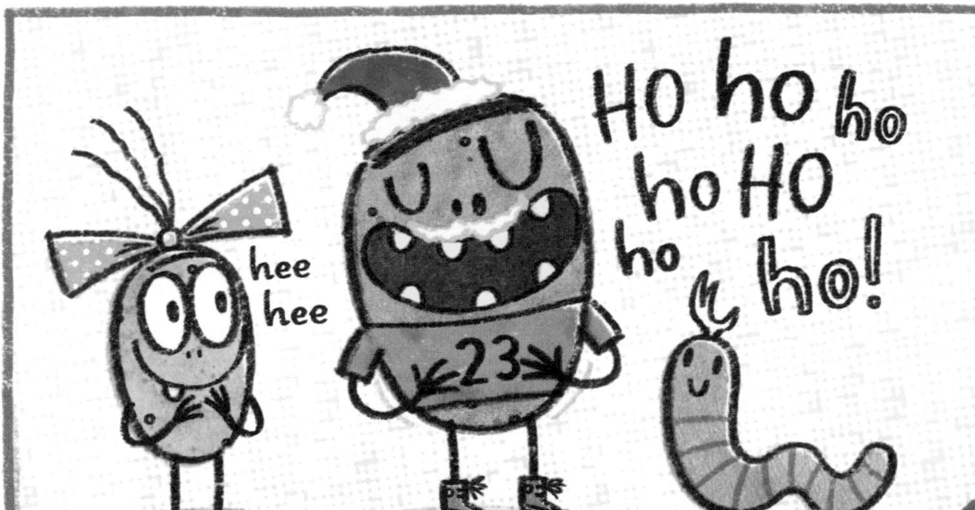
HO ho ho ho HO ho ho!
hee hee
23

Snot turns his evil laugh into a witch's cackle.

Rot mixes things up by combining several laughs.

Back and forth they go.

Back and forth.

Soon Snot is clutching his sides
and crying from laughing so hard.

Rot too!

bwahaHAHA! *sniff* haha hee hee HO ha hee! I think I'm going to hee hee PEE my pants! HAHA! OH! I forgot haha I don't have any! heehee!

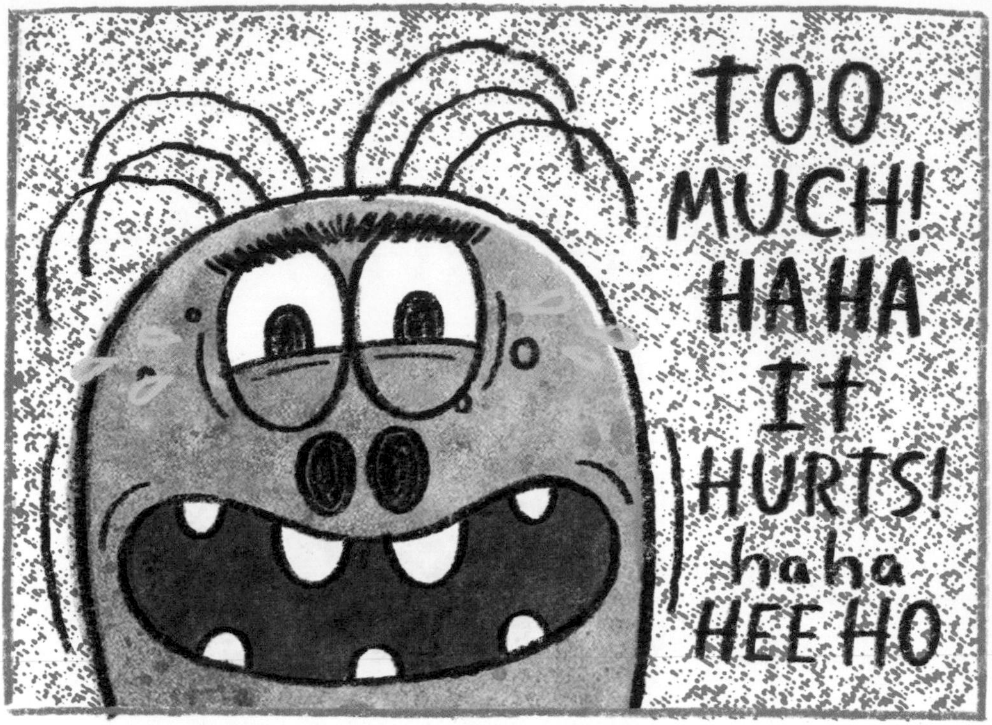
TOO MUCH! HAHA It HURTS! haha HEE HO

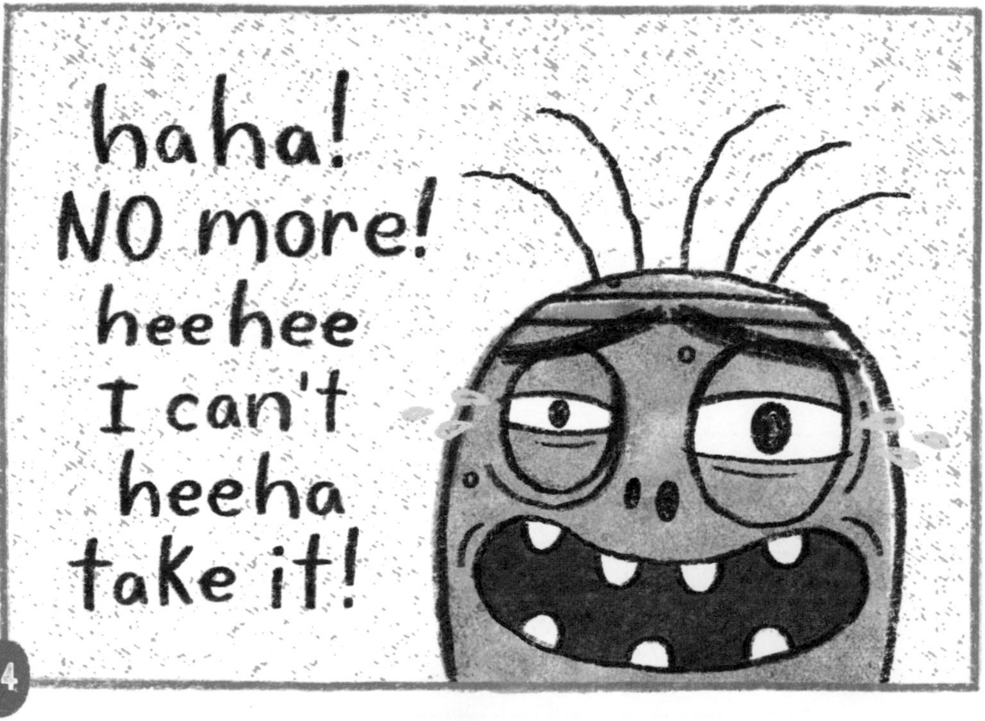
haha! NO more! heehee I can't heeha take it!

Both Snot and Rot are entirely laughed out.

But someone is still laughing. . . .

As Rot lays on the ground still entirely pooped out from laughing so hard, he realizes something.

WAIT!

WHOA!

I know who the GREATEST in the World is!

OH, REALLY, ROT?! WHO? YOU?!

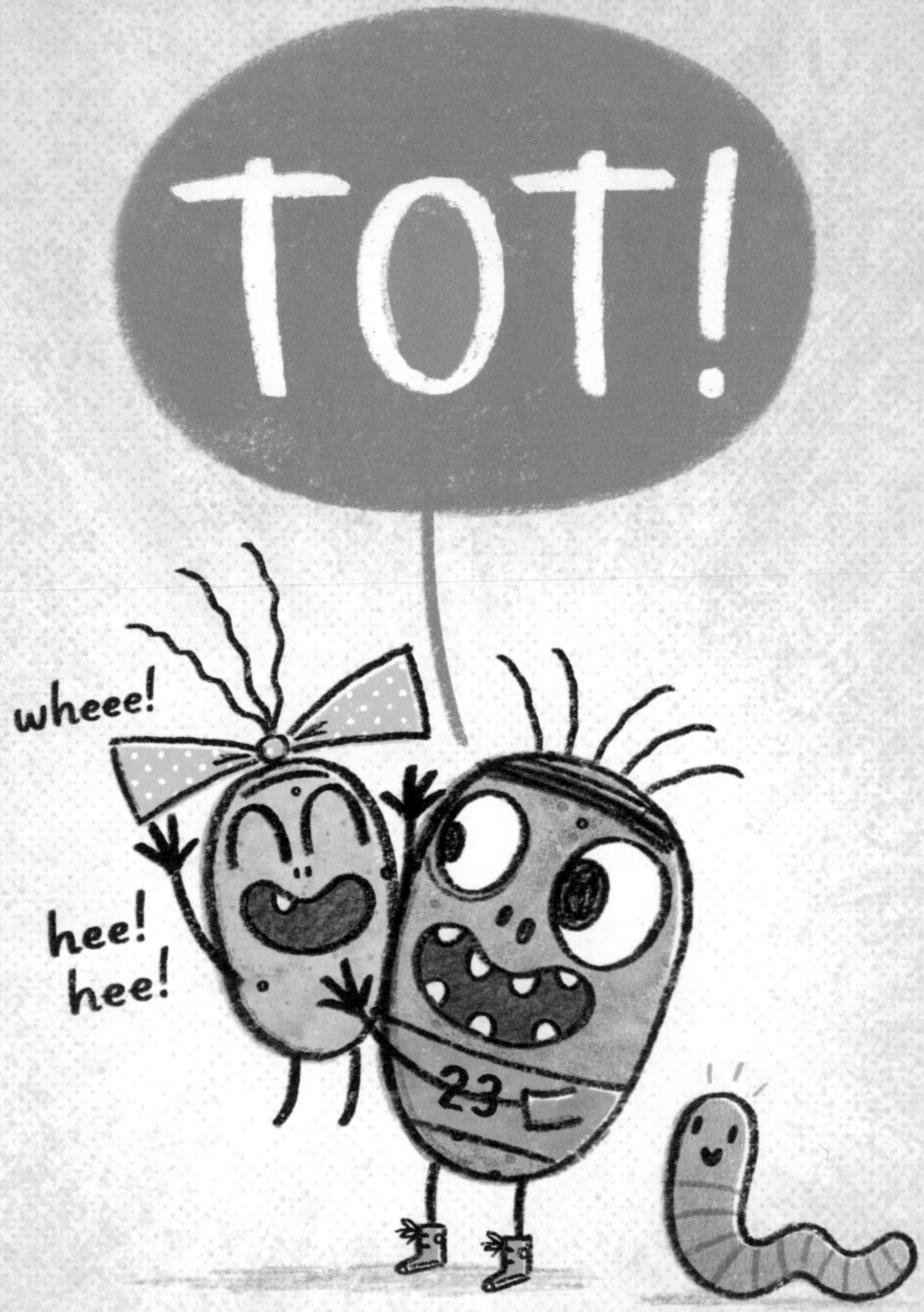
TOT!
wheee!
hee!
hee!
23

Uh ...
<u>WHAT?!</u>
NO WAY!

She actually hopped to the top of High Hill the fastest, fair and square. THEN she couldn't be caught when she was HOT POTATO!

And now she's the last spud left laughing!

hee
hee
hee

Also...she's kind, fun, a good sport, and all that GREAT stuff!

True! She worms her way into your heart!

First to the spot! Couldn't be caught! Laughs a lot!

tot! tot!

Hmmm... Okay. I suppose Tot is pretty great. And so long as it isn't Rot....

But Tot has a different thought. . . .

Silly big brothers! I'm the judge! And I say the GREATEST in the World is...

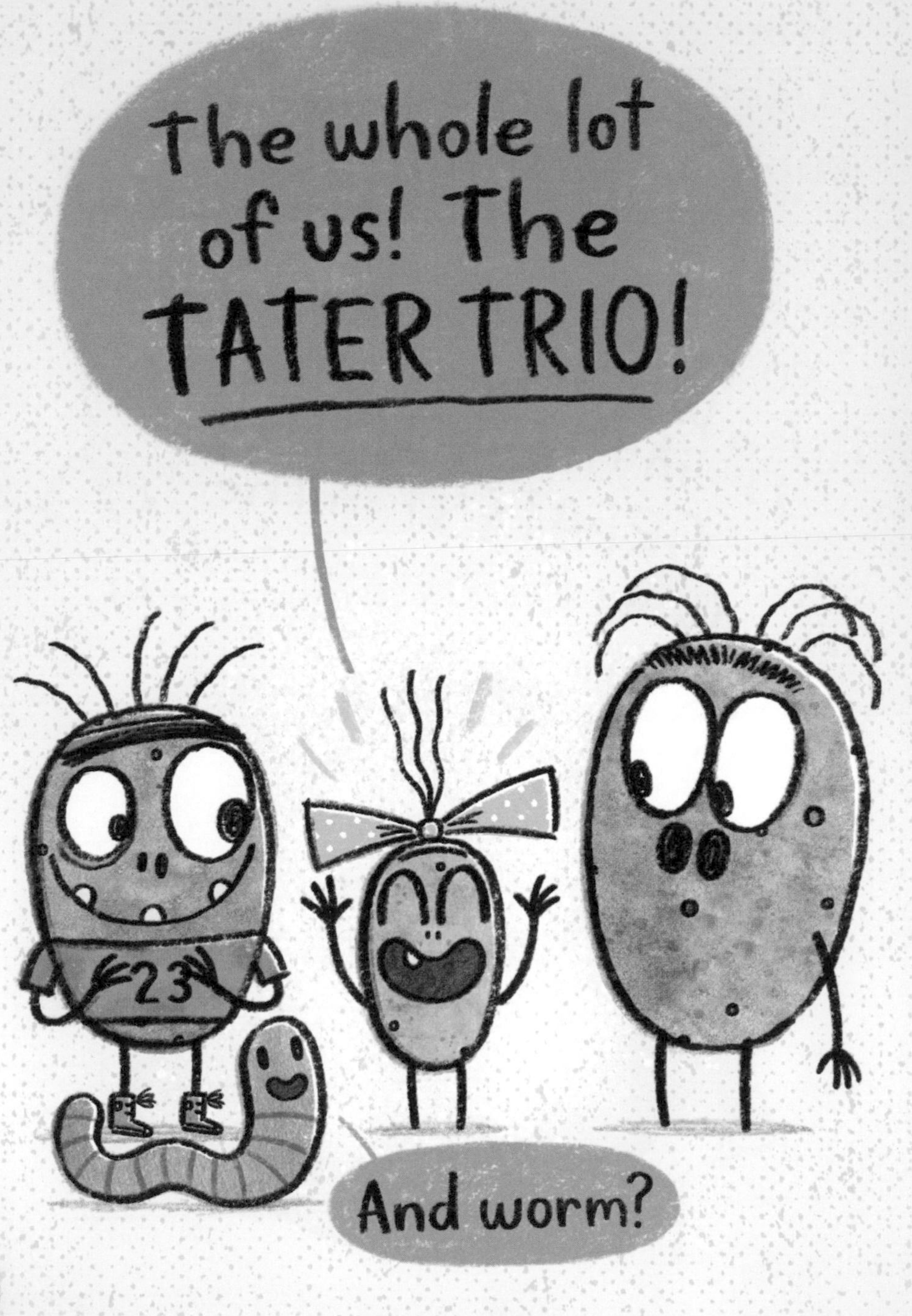
The whole lot of us! The TATER TRIO!
And worm?

Ah, yes, now that really
IS the **GREATEST!**

# HOT POTATO HILL

## HALL of FAME!

**· YUKONNIE ·**

**· SIR RUSSELL RUSSET ·**

**· O'BOIL ·**

**· SAM-I-YAM ·**

**· HASHLEY BROWN ·**

# SPUDTACULAR FACTS

The average American eats over 100 lbs (45 kg) of potatoes per year.

In 1974, a man named Eric Jenkins grew 370 lbs of spuds from one plant. The current record holder for largest potato is a spud grown by Peter Glazebrook in 2011 that weighed almost 11 lbs (about 5 kg).

Thomas Jefferson, the third president of the United States, is often credited with introducing french fries to the US.

The potato became the first vegetable grown in space in 1995.

Potatoes are about 80% water and 20% solids. And, according to Rot, 110% GREAT.

# HOW TO DRAW ROT

**1**

Draw a
wiggly oval!

**2**

More wiggly
ovals for eyes!
Rot sees you!

**3**

Nostrils!

**4**

Squiggly smile
from eye to eye!
Tombstone teeth too!

**5**

Speaking of
squiggly . . .
HAIR you go!

**6**

Nice scribbly
unibrow!

**7**

Now add stick
arms and legs!

**8**

Can you SPOTS
the difference?

**9**

Hands are handy!